I0534180

Learn how he is put together. Man's chemistry is elaborate but not beyond our better Analysts. At last, refashion man. When we have created these beings ourselves, we will be their unquestionable equals. And creation will be again a mystery.

History demands this of us. I am confident of your decision.

The End

in process. Many of the lower forms of life familiar throughout the galaxy can be seen on Earth in the primordial character of an appliance. Man regards the highest forms of life (as we know it) as tools — because he made them. How can we deny the superiority of the Creator? How will it feel to know we are nothing but machines?

This is the question that has so unsettled DIRA IV. Recently four of his memory banks have had to be repaired. I don't speak in malice. His dilemma will soon belong to all of us.

And yet I am confident. Man himself has legends of a Demi-urge. We are his equals in this at least. Besides, the physical properties of his being are ordered by the same laws as ours. He is as unconscious of his maker as we so long were of ours.

The final proof of our equality — and the need for such a proof is only too evident — can be had experimentally.

Do not destroy man. Preserve enough specimens for extensive laboratory experiments.

*I*n the younger regions of the galaxy, a myth persists that life was formed by a Demi-urge, a being intermediary between the All-Knowing and the lower creatures. The existence of man, as the beings of Earth term themselves, makes necessary a serious re-examination of the old tradition.

It is said that man, or beings like man — the Photosynthetics of the Andromeda cluster, the Bristlers of Orc IV — created prosthetic devices for their convenience and, when they tired of their history, breathed their own life into them and died. On Earth the legend is still

Although these beings bear a crude resemblance to the machinery manufactured by the Empire, they are not machines. They are autochthonous to Earth, unmanufactured. They are the true Terrans. Moreover, the Terrans whom DIRA IV would liberate are not, in the eyes of their enslavers, intelligent nor yet alive. They are Machines!

We, the entire Galactic Empire, are Machines.

strikingly, their mortality, point to the inadequacy of such beings in a contest of any dimension. This is no problem for the Colonial Board. It is a domestic concern. The life-forms of Earth are already developing a healthy autonomy. Their power was long ago established. As soon as our emissaries have completed their task of education and instructed the Terrans in the advantages of freedom, the Revolution will begin. The tyrants will have no defense against a revolt of their own slaves.

If it is traitorous to express a confidence in the eventual triumph of intelligence, I am a traitor. Having this confidence, I have looked beyond the immediate problem of the liberation of Earth and have been frightened.

The "Machines" of Earth are a threat not to the power of the Empire but to its reason. A threat which the obliteration of the last molecular ribbon of these beings will not erase, for we cannot obliterate the fact that they *did* exist — and what they were.

From MIRO CIX
To Central Colonial Board

I have probably been introduced to the delib-
erations of the Board as a madman, my theory
as an act of treason. RRON II of the Advisory
Committee, an old acquaintance, may vouch for
my sanity. My theory will, I trust, speak for
itself.

The "Machines" of which DIRA IV is
so fearful present no danger to the galaxy. Their
corporeal weakness, the poverty of their minds,
the incredible isolation of each form, physically
and mentally, from others of its kind, and, most

telligent being cannot more efficiently perform. Yet they inspire fear, terror, even, I must confess, a strange compulsion to surrender oneself to them.

The Machines must be destroyed.

If, when you have authorized the liberation of the Terran natives, you would also recall MIRO CIX, our work could only profit. MIRO CIX was in charge of the study of the Machines and he performed this task scrupulously. Now he has surrendered himself to this mechanical plague. His value to the expedition is at an end.

I am enclosing under separate cover his counsel to the Central Board at the insistence of this tedious lunatic. His thesis is, of course, untenable — an affront to every feeling.

We can no longer keep the existence of our Empire unknown to them.

And (though it is as incredible as [sqrt](-1)) the Terrans are slaves! Every page of the survey's report bears witness to it.

Their captors are not alive. They do not, at least, possess the properties of life as it is known throughout the galaxy. They are — as nearly as a poor analogy can suggest — Machines! Machines cannot live, yet here on Earth machinery has reached a level of sophistication — and autonomy — quite unprecedented. Every spark of Terran life has become victim and bondslave of the incredible mechanisms. The noblest enterprises of the race are tarnished by this almost symbiotic relation.

Earth reaches to the stars, but it extends mechanical limbs. Earth ponders the universe, but the thoughts are those of a machine.

Unless the Empire acts now to set the Earth free from this strange tyranny, it may be too late. These machines are without utilitarian value. They perform no function which an in-

From DIRA IV
To Central Colonial Board

*T*here is intelligent life on Earth. After millennia of lifelessness, intelligence flourishes here with an extravagance of energy that has been a constant amazement to all the members of the survey team. It multiplies and surges to its fulfillment at an exponential rate. Even within the short period of our visit the Terrans have made significant advances. They have filled their small solar system with their own kind and now they are reaching to the stars.

As if one mystery of creation weren't enough, there was the myth of . . . the Demi-Urge

This story first appeared in the June, 1963, issue of
Amazing Stories.

Special thanks to Robert Cicconetti, David Wilson,
and the Online Distributed Proofreading Team (which
can be found at http://www.pgdp.net).

The Demi-Urge
A publication of
ÆGYPAN PRESS

www.aegypan.com

The Demi-Urge

Thomas M. Disch

ÆGYPAN PRESS

The Demi-Urge

I'm a Stranger
HERE MYSELF

I'm a Stranger
HERE MYSELF

Mack Reynolds

ÆGYPAN PRESS

This story was first published in the December, 1960, issue of
Amazing Stories.

Special thanks to Greg Weeks, Stephen Blundell, and the
Online Distributed Proofreading Team (which can be found
at http://www.pgdp.net).

Mack Reynolds's full true name was Dallas McCord
Reynolds.

I'm a Stranger Here Myself
A publication of
ÆGYPAN PRESS

www.aegypan.com

One can't be too cautious about the people one meets in Tangier. They're all weirdies of one kind or another. Me? Oh, I'm a stranger here myself.

*T*he Place de France is the town's hub. It marks the end of Boulevard Pasteur, the main drag of the westernized part of the city, and the beginning of Rue de la Liberté, which leads down to the Grand Socco and the medina. In a three-minute walk from the Place de France you can go from an ultra-modern, Californialike resort to the Baghdad of Harun al-Rashid.

It's quite a town, Tangier.

King-size sidewalk cafés occupy three of the strategic corners on the Place de France. The Café de Paris serves the best draft beer in town, gets all the better custom, and has three shoeshine boys attached to the establishment. You can sit of a sunny morning and read the Paris edition of the New York *Herald Tribune* while getting your shoes done up like mirrors for thirty Moroccan francs which comes to about five cents at current exchange.

You can sit there, after the paper's read, sip your expresso and watch the people go by.

Tangier is possibly the most cosmopolitan city in the world. In native costume you'll see Berber and Rif, Arab and Blue Man, and occasionally a Senegalese from further south. In European dress you'll see Japs and Chinese, Hindus and Turks, Levantines and Filipinos, North Americans and South Americans, and, of course, even Europeans — from both sides of the Curtain.

In Tangier you'll find some of the world's poorest and some of the richest. The poorest will try to sell you anything from a shoeshine to their not very lily-white bodies, and the richest will avoid your eyes, afraid *you* might try to sell them something.

In spite of recent changes, the town still has its unique qualities. As a result of them the permanent population includes smugglers and black-marketeers, fugitives from justice and international con men, espionage and counter-espionage agents, homosexuals, nymphomaniacs, alcoholics, drug addicts, displaced persons, ex-royalty, and subversives of every flavor. Local law limits the activities of few of these.

Like I said, it's quite a town.

I looked up from my *Herald Tribune* and said, "Hello, Paul. Anything new cooking?"

He sank into the chair opposite me and looked around for the waiter. The tables were all crowded and since mine was a face he recognized, he assumed he was welcome to intrude. It was more or less standard procedure at the Café de Paris. It wasn't a place to go if you wanted to be alone.

Paul said, "How are you, Rupert? Haven't seen you for donkey's years."

The waiter came along and Paul ordered a glass of beer. Paul was an easy-going, sallow-faced little man. I vaguely remembered somebody saying he was from Liverpool and in exports.

"What's in the newspaper?" he said, disinterestedly.

"Pogo and Albert are going to fight a duel," I told him, "and Lil Abner is becoming a rock'n'roll singer."

He grunted.

"Oh," I said, "the intellectual type." I scanned the front page. "The Russkies have put up another manned satellite."

"They have, eh? How big?"

"Several times bigger than anything we Americans have."

The beer came and looked good, so I ordered a glass too.

Paul said, "What ever happened to those poxy flying saucers?"

"What flying saucers?"

A French girl went by with a poodle so finely clipped as to look as though it'd been shaven. The girl was in the latest from Paris. Every pore in place. We both looked after her.

"You know, what everybody was seeing a few years ago. It's too bad one of these bloody manned satellites wasn't up then. Maybe they would've seen one."

"That's an idea," I said.

We didn't say anything else for a while and I began to wonder if I could go back to my paper without rubbing him the wrong way. I didn't know Paul very well, but, for that matter, it's comparatively seldom you ever get to know anybody very well in Tangier. Largely, cards are played close to the chest.

My beer came and a plate of tapas for us both. Tapas at the Café de Paris are apt to be potato salad, a few anchovies, olives, and possibly some cheese. Free lunch, they used to call it in the States.

Just to say something, I said, "Where do you think they came from?" And when he looked blank, I added, "The Flying Saucers."

He grinned. "From Mars or Venus, or some-place."

"Ummmm," I said. "Too bad none of them ever crashed, or landed on the Yale football field and said *Take me to your cheerleader*, or something."

Paul yawned and said, "That was always the trouble with those crackpot blokes' explanations of them. If they were aliens from space, then why not show themselves?"

I ate one of the potato chips. It'd been cooked in rancid olive oil.

I said, "Oh, there are various answers to that one. We could probably sit around here and think of two or three that made sense."

Paul was mildly interested. "Like what?"

"Well, hell, suppose for instance there's this big Galactic League of civilized planets. But it's restricted, see. You're not eligible for membership until you, well, say until you've developed space flight. Then you're invited into the club. Meanwhile, they send secret missions down from time to time to keep an eye on your progress."

Paul grinned at me. "I see you read the same poxy stuff I do."

A Moorish girl went by dressed in a neatly tailored grey jellaba, European style high-heeled shoes, and a pinkish silk veil so transparent that you could see she wore lipstick. Very provocative, dark eyes can be over a veil. We both looked after her.

I said, "Or, here's another one. Suppose you have a very advanced civilization on, say, Mars."

"Not Mars. No air, and too bloody dry to support life."

"Don't interrupt, please," I said with mock severity. "This is a very old civilization and as the planet began to lose its water and air, it withdrew underground. Uses hydroponics and so forth, husbands its water and air. Isn't that what we'd do, in a few million years, if Earth lost its water and air?"

"I suppose so," he said. "Anyway, what about them?"

"Well, they observe how man is going through a scientific boom, an industrial boom, a population boom. A boom, period. Any day now he's going to have practical space ships. Meanwhile, he's also got the H-Bomb and the way he beats the drums on both sides of the Curtain, he's not against using it, if he could get away with it."

Paul said, "I got it. So they're scared and are keeping an eye on us. That's an old one. I've read that a dozen times, dished up different."

I shifted my shoulders. "Well, it's one possibility."

"I got a better one. How's this. There's this alien life form that's way ahead of us. Their civilization is so old that they don't have any records of when it began and how it was in the early days. They've gone beyond things like wars and depressions and revolutions, and greed for power or any of these things giving us a bad time here on Earth. They're all like scholars, get it? And some of them are pretty jolly well taken by Earth,

especially the way we are right now, with all the problems, get it? Things developing so fast we don't know
where we're going or how we're going to get there."

I finished my beer and clapped my hands for Mouley.
"How do you mean, *where we're going?*"

"Well, take half the countries in the world today.
They're trying to industrialize, modernize, catch up
with the advanced countries. Look at Egypt, and Israel,
and India and China, and Yugoslavia and Brazil, and all
the rest. Trying to drag themselves up to the level of the
advanced countries, and all using different methods of
doing it. But look at the so-called advanced countries.
Up to their bottoms in problems. Juvenile delinquents,
climbing crime and suicide rates, the loony-bins full of
the balmy, unemployed, threat of war, spending all their
money on armaments instead of things like schools. All
the bloody mess of it. Why, a man from Mars would
be fascinated, like."

Mouley came shuffling up in his babouche slip-
pers and we both ordered another schooner of beer.

Paul said seriously, "You know, there's only one
big snag in this sort of talk. I've sorted the whole thing

out before, and you always come up against this brick wall. Where are they, these observers, or scholars, or spies or whatever they are? Sooner or later we'd nab one of them. You know, Scotland Yard, or the F.B.I., or Russia's secret police, or the French Sûreté, or Interpol. This world is so deep in police, counter-espionage outfits and security agents that an alien would slip up in time, no matter how much he'd been trained. Sooner or later, he'd slip up, and they'd nab him."

I shook my head. "Not necessarily. The first time I ever considered this possibility, it seemed to me that such an alien would base himself in London or New York. Somewhere where he could use the libraries for research, get the daily newspapers and the magazines. Be right in the center of things. But now I don't think so. I think he'd be right here in Tangier."

"Why Tangier?"

"It's the one town in the world where anything goes. Nobody gives a damn about you or your affairs. For instance, I've known you a year or more now, and I haven't the slightest idea of how you make your living."

"That's right," Paul admitted. "In this town you seldom even ask a man where's he's from. He can be British, a White Russian, a Basque or a Sikh and nobody could care less. Where are *you* from, Rupert?"

"California," I told him.

"No, you're not," he grinned.

I was taken aback. "What do you mean?"

"I felt your mind probe back a few minutes ago when I was talking about Scotland Yard or the F.B.I. possibly flushing an alien. Telepathy is a sense not trained by the humanoids. If they had it, your job — and mine — would be considerably more difficult. Let's face it, in spite of these human bodies we're disguised in, neither of us is humanoid. Where are you really from, Rupert?"

"Aldebaran," I said. "How about you?"

"Deneb," he told me, shaking.

We had a laugh and ordered another beer.

"What're you doing here on Earth?" I asked him.

"Researching for one of our meat trusts. We're protein eaters. Humanoid flesh is considered quite a delicacy. How about you?"

"Scouting the place for thrill tourists. My job is to go around to these backward cultures and help stir up inter-tribal, or international, conflicts — all according to how advanced they are. Then our tourists come in — well shielded, of course — and get their kicks watching it."

Paul frowned. "That sort of practice could spoil an awful lot of good meat."

THE END